Justice Is Inevitable

Justice Is Inevitable

The Pursuit of Justice in the Shadow

Odo Evaristus Ikechukwu

EXCELLER BOOKS®
A GLOBAL PRESS

Justice Is Inevitable
The Pursuit of Justice in the Shadow

Cover design by Exceller Books using resources from Pixabay.com

ISBN: 978-81-19524-60-0

First published in India in 2025 by Exceller Books
Address: G1, Dream Apartment, Degree College Road, Belgharia, Kolkata, 700056, India
www.excellerbooks.com

EXCELLER BOOKS®
A GLOBAL PRESS

Dedication

My father, late Mr. John Uwakwe Odo &
My mother, late Mrs. Josephine nwakaego Odo

Acknowledgement

I would like to thank my Wife, Mrs Uwakwe Victoria Nwaneka, for her support and encouragement. My three children, Sophia, Bede and Elvis, whose interests in my storytelling motivated me to take up the project.

Looking from the hilltop of Kinsama city, you will see the whole town radiating from the well-planned landscape and highly articulated streetlights glowing in different colours. Legend has it that the European coal miners built the city. You can see the evidence in the type of architecture scattered around the town, especially within the coastal line of the Kinsama River. Initially, the people of the Igigbo tribe, whose main occupation, by most of their men, was farming, inhabited the city. It is the culture of the Igigbo to take good care of their wives. Their women mostly stay at home to take care of the hut and cook for their men and children. They believe that women should not suffer; instead, they are to look good and be happy. The first European settlers met the culture and liked it. The Igigbos are accommodating in nature, which gave the Europeans more courage to mingle with the indigenes freely. The Europeans employed them as either gardeners or cleaners. Some of them employed two or more workers because they lived in big houses with a large compound surrounded by a well-cultured garden. It is said that the noise of lawnmowers from all the European quarters used to fill the air in the early mornings on Saturdays. Those who did not mow their lawn were busy jogging around the street with their dogs. The indigenes and the servants usually came out to have a look at them. Even after the Europeans have gone, the city still maintains its serene nature: beautiful and clean. This beauty makes Kinsama enjoy the inflow of tourists from all over the world. Apart from agriculture, tourism gives them over 40% of their gross domestic earning.

The city airport lies within fifteen kilometres of the town. It is one of the busiest airports in the country. Now and then, numerous aeroplanes take off and land, bringing a lot of tourists and business people into the city. Especially during the weekend, holidaymakers fill the city. This inflow of people has made Kinsama's residents indulge in businesses like hotels, restaurants, fashion, and design using local fabrics. There is a saying that if you want to catch some dollars, go to Kinsama.

***

No 7 Kinsama Boulevard is a seven-apartment block housing both business and civil servants. Each apartment has two bedrooms, all in a suite, one living room, a kitchen, and a balcony facing the road. The gallery is designed with a concrete art block wall and furnished with a cast iron rod that makes it impossible for someone walking on the road to see the occupants relaxing on the balcony. During the hot weather, the occupants, with their various resting materials, always make use of the balcony to relax and enjoy the fresh air. When Gudy was shown the house by the estate agent handling the building, he did not waste time but paid in full for one year's rent. He told the agent that he was new in town, an investor, and there was a business he wanted to start in Kinsama City. The apartment was mainly for his staff, who would be managing the business. After signing some documents, the agent thanked Gudy for doing business with him and left.

Gudy sat and lit his Cuba cigar, thinking of what Darrel told him about Edyta. He looked across the road and saw the neatly constructed bungalow, which she told him was built and owned by his enemy. Gudy took up his Samsung Galaxy phone and took some pictures of the bungalow. He was satisfied with his shot. Soon after, he dialled a number. The other end simply said, "I have been waiting for your call, sir." Gudy replied, "Meet me at no 7 Kinsama Boulevard Pronto," and ended the call. Then, he looked at the bungalow again, shook his head, and waited for his visitor.

***

Trench was a tall and slim fighter who used every weapon at his disposal when fighting. When walking, he hardly made any sound, a gait pattern that gave him the nickname 'the cat'. He had been meditating on the call he received from his old friend Gudy. For over six months now, he had not heard from him. He remembered the incident that led to their separation in different ways in the Contuoo region. Was it why Gudy was calling him? Gudy was brief with his call. He simply said, "Find some time this week and meet me in Kinsama City, as I have a surprise for you." What kind of surprise did his old friend Gudy have for him? Why Kinsama? He had never been to the place before, but he learned that the area is a beautiful holiday destination for tourists. But he was not in the mood for any holiday. He had some businesses he was pushing, which he needed to give attention to. Should he call back his friend to ask for more time before coming? He knew whatever might have made Gudy invite him to Kinsama must be serious business. He decided to give him a try. He picked up his phone and dialled his flight agent's number; the agent picked up the phone at once, and he said, "Book a one-way ticket for me to Kinsama City on the weekend."

"Yes, sir. Would you like business class or economy class, sir?" the agent asked.

"Business class will do; send me the amount, your account number, and confirmation number as soon as you are through," he replied.

"Consider it done, sir," assured the agent.

He cut the call, stood up to pick up his car key, and looked at himself in the mirror.

"I need to shave, and I have to look good meeting my old friend," he said to himself.

He entered his car and sped towards one of the barber's shops along his street.

As Gudy was watching the bungalow, one saloon car stopped in front of his apartment block. He saw Spyker coming out of the vehicle. He brought out his phone and dialled his number. As soon as Spyker picked up the phone, he ordered Spyker, "Come up to apartment 3b."

"Yes, sir," Spyker replied.

He turned off the phone as Spyker entered the House and briefed him on what he wanted him to do.

"I have arranged all you need to survive for two months; please give me a perfect job with no mistakes."

After saying this, he left, went into the parking lot, got into his Range Rover SUV, which he had bought three days ago, and hit the road to his hotel, where he was staying at the moment. He knew that Darrel would be waiting for him.

Sharon was a very tall, good-looking young girl aged between 20 and 25. She looked like a high-model school girl. Her shape was like that of a good piece of woodwork.

She was a media personality who, every morning between 6.30 and 7.00, to keep herself fit, jogged around neatly paved streets within the neighbourhood in a well-dressed up-and-down jogger with Nike canvas to match. The neighbours, both married and unmarried, admired her. There were one or two occasions when some of her admirers met with an accident when they forgot that they were on the steering wheel. Girls and married women had to strongly warn their boyfriends and husbands not to look in her direction.

She worked with a famous media outfit in town. Her job was mainly to interview tourists to find out where they came from and what motivated them to visit the country.

Finishing his university studies with a BSc in Art, Jordyn drew so well that most of his friends and lovers of his work compared him to Picasso. His paintings were like pictures taken by perfect photography in a well-articulated studio.

He dreamed big of going full-time into painting and organizing exhibitions once in a while to showcase his talent. But all this required a lot of money, which he did not have.

***

Coming back to her apartment after jogging, Sharon took her bath and dressed in some lovely attire. She looked at the mirror and felt satisfied. The weather was so bright that there was no need to go with an umbrella, but she decided to take it in case the weather changed. She had only an hour to attend to her job. The previous day, she informed her boss that she would have an old-time visitor. She entered her car and drove straight to catch some of the tourists who were just new in town. She drove to the popular tourist hotel in the town where she usually met and interact with the tourists with her cameraman.

As she entered the hotel lobby, she saw the receptionist, and both of them exchanged pleasantries. The receptionist was busy admiring her attire and wanted to know where she made her clothes and what diet she was on. As they were talking, she noticed an unfamiliar face, and because of her training, she knew immediately that he was a tourist. She beckoned to her cameraman to come along.

Spyker had been working for Gudy for five years now. He knew that what Gudy hated so much was a failure. He is determined to carry out that assignment so discretely. He wondered why Gudy brought him to Kinsama City to watch bungalows. Spyker had already received part of his fees two days ago, so he had nothing to lose. All he knew he would be missing was his girl. But he told her that he would be back as soon as possible. Now and then, he was watching the building with his binoculars. He only saw the man he believed was the gateman and no one else. Then he went to the kitchen to make himself lunch.

***

Jordyn woke up very early, dressed in casual jean trousers and a t-shirt, and prayed as he had never done before. He had an interview with one of the lovers of his work who invited him to his office. Jordyn knew that Edyta had money, and if Edyta wished, he could help him sponsor the exhibition of his work. As he stepped into the lavishly furnished office room of Edyta, what came into his mind was that this man was dam so rich that if he handled him well, he might play ball. Edyta greeted him and ushered him to a seat. He sat down, admiring the office. Edyta allowed him to feed his eyes, pretending to be searching for a file in the file cabinet. Looking through his shoulder, he saw Jordyn admiring his office. He knew right in his mind that he caught him.

Before the thought faded, Sharon stepped in and greeted her new tourist. She was good with words, apart from her look. Sharon had a good command of the English language. Within some minutes, she hypnotized the tourist. She collected all she needed to know about the man and promised to call back if need be.

Edyta was a notorious drug dealer and '419' man who mainly used the office to cover his evil dealings. He had one staff, who happened to be his girlfriend, as a secretary. As Jordyn sat down, he offered him a glass of gin, which he took. He took a sip and thanked him for the drink and also for inviting him to his office.

Edyta told him that he had many international friends to whom he had shown his work, and they were so much in love with his paintings. He wanted him to work harder and come back to the office with many good paintings in two days because some of his business partners would be in town. He believed that if he came up with good work, his business partners would take over his exhibition costs.

After about 30 minutes, Sharon was through with her tourist guy. She discharged the cameraman because she was due to go to the airport to pick up Cendy, who happened to be her bosom friend back in her school days.

They were so fond of each other that back in their school days, their classmates called them unfortunate twins.

As she zoomed her baby towards Kinsama Airport Road, she smiled, thinking of what the tourist had told her about how beautiful and sexy she was. If Sharon had granted his request, he would have liked to know more about her. She went to the pigeonhole of her car, picked up her Gucci designer sunglasses, put them on, and looked in the mirror. She liked what she saw. Without thinking much of the tourist, she stepped on the throttle of her car and increased the speed.

Jordyn was highly impressed with what Edyta told him. He promised him that in two days, he would not be disappointed with what he was going to see. Edyta opened the drawer, brought some bundles of two hundred naira notes, and gave them to Jordyn. He collected them with many thanks.

***

It was 10.30 in the morning, and there was not much traffic on the road to the airport. Her friend's flight would be landing by 11 am if there was no delay, according to the information Cendy sent to her. Plus or minus, she would make it to the airport on time. As she was admiring herself in the mirror of her car, she failed to notice a sharp stone in the middle of the road. Her front tyre missed the stone, but the back tyre was not so lucky. Being a good driver, Sharon controlled the car perfectly well and parked it by the side of the road, thinking about the accident that could have happened and her friend, Cendy.

As Jordyn stepped into his house, he narrated the event of the day to his roommate, an undercover policeman. His name was Tony. With his heavily built structure, he looked like a gym instructor. Girls loved his shape so much that whenever he went to nightclubs, he had many girls to dance with. He is not yet married, but hopefully, he was ready to marry if he found a girl of her dreams.

As Jordyn told him where he went and whom he met, little did he know that Tony had been working on Edyta? Within the police community, Edyta's notorious activities were well-known. However, the only problem was that they had no evidence to hook him in most of the crimes the police believed he was the chief architect of.

Tony was so interested in knowing more about Edyta. However, his friend Jordyn did not understand why he was so interested in Edyta, especially as he did not know Edyta much.

He only saw him as a successful businessman who he believed would help him achieve his aim.

At precisely 11 am, Cendy's flight touched the ground, ran through the runway, reversed and parked on the tarmac. As she came out of the flight, Cendy breathed in the fresh air, admiring herself carrying her Gucci bag loosely on her shoulder, and cat-walked towards the arrival hall.

She collected her bag from the conveyor belt in the arrival hall. One of the airport staff members attended her. She gave him her boarding pass with baggage slip on it. At a glance, the staff gave her a nod and allowed her to go.

Sharon was now in a real state of quagmire. She did not know what to do. She looked right and left; the nearest garage was about 6km. She opened her handbag, and to her face, her phone was not there. She forgot to plug out the phone where she was charging it in the tourist hotel. There was no way she could reach her friend Cendy. The only option was to find a cab, but the problem was that not many taxis would be available on the road at 11 am because it was not the rush hour. She waited and waited, thinking of what her friend must be going through.

As Cendy stepped out of the airport's waiting area, she looked for her friends but could not find her. She unzipped her Gucci bag and brought out her iPhone 10 to dial Sharon's number, but to her surprise, there was no answer. She dialled it several more times, but there was no answer. She was now anxious. She remembered that before they board, she had called her, and they spoke. What might have been the problem? As she was contemplating what to do, she failed to notice one handsome young man following her at her back.

Pete was one of Edyta's boys whose main job was to look for stranded visitor in town to his master, Edyta.

He was a graduate of mass communication. He spoke very well and always put on a charming smile to attract his prey.

He stepped in and said, "Madam, is everything okay? You look worried. I have been watching you from a distance and noticed that everything is not right with you. My name is Pettier, but my friends call me Pete. What is your name? And if all is not well with you, would you mind sharing it with me? Let me see if I can be of help."

Cendy looked at him and saw him as a harmless guy. She knew that Sharon had told her about bad boys in town who go about kidnapping young girls. But looking at this young guy standing in front of her, she was pretty sure he was not one of them. Besides, she did not know what might have happened to Sharon. She decided to give him a trial. "I'm Cendy. This is my first time in this town, and I came to see my friend. I have been calling her number but to no avail. She is not picking up her phone. Before boarding the plane, I called her, and we talked. Only God knows why Sharon wants to welcome me in this manner."

***

After standing in the hot sun for more than 25 minutes, Sharon finally saw one cabman. She jumped into the car without wasting time, praying she would catch up with her friend in peace.

***

"You mean Sharon, the media woman?" Pete said to Cendy. Cendy's face brightened up a little bit.

"Do you know her?" asked Cendy.

"Come on, who doesn't know Sharon in this city. Not only do I know her, but I also know where she lives. I can take you to her house if you don't mind," said Pete.

Cendy was so relieved. She simply said, "Please take me to her. I will simply kill her for abandoning me like this."

Pete helped her with her bag while going to the parking lot. Sharon failed to notice a man and a woman walking toward one Avalon Toyota car as she stepped out of her cab. She ran out of the cab and went into the waiting area, but no one greeted her except a few workers and a few passengers waiting for their invitees. She ran back to the cab, and the only option for her was to go back to the tourist hotel to pick up her phone so she could call her.

In a hurry, Tony dressed up, went into the kitchen to get juice from the fridge and drank a glass of it. Closing the door, he put the call across to his boss and left.

Tim was an intelligent police officer with an excellent record. He had worked on many cases, especially on kidnapping and drug-related cases. He knew that Tony calling him at that time meant that he had useful information for him. Taking his automatic police gun, he dashed out of his office. They usually met at a cheap bar outside the city.

As Pete was driving slowly, he pushed the radio button of his car. The melodious music of Bob Marley (one love) filled the car. He said to Cendy, "In less than 20 minutes, you will be with your friend."

Cendy thanked him for coming to her rescue. In his usually charming voice, he told Cendy about the beautiful areas of the town where she would ask her friend Sharon to take her to the best restaurants and the newly opened cinema in town.

Cendy was so captivated by the way this man talked that, in her mind, she had already developed a soft spot for him and would like to see him again.

At 11.45 am, Sharon's cab pulled over at the parking lot of the tourist hotel. She opened the cab door and moved at an alarming speed towards the hotel's reception area. This time, there was no room for pleasantries. At the corner of the hotel lobby, she sighted the receptionist dressed in faded blue jeans, trousers and a t-shirt. She was already on her way out after working all night. "Sophie! My phone, please," she said as she moved towards the lobby.

"Is anything the matter? I gave the phone to the storekeeper."

She walked past Sophie, breathing heavily, and opened the storekeeper's door without knocking.

"My phone, please."

"Sharon, what is the matter?" the storekeeper asked.

"I'm not in the mood for all these questions. Please, I need my phone." Without wasting time, she opened the drawer of her office table and handed the phone to her.

A little bit relaxed, she switched on the phone.

Edyta, having received a short message from Pete (The bird is in the nest), knew precisely what Pete meant. He instructed his secretary to lock up his office that he had an urgent business that needed his attention. Carrying his briefcase, he walked towards his parking lot. Edyta was a person who liked a good life. He had a lot of exotic cars, but that day, he came to the office with his latest collection, the Prado Toyota SUV. He admired the car, opened the door, entered and adjusted the seat of the SUV. He slotted the ignition key and started the vehicle as the gateman opened the gate. He carefully entered the road leading to one of his guest houses, which he purposely built to keep his prey. He dialled a number, and at the other end of the phone, a lady's voice greeted him.

"Meet me at the guest house, Pronto," he told the lady, put down his phone and focused on the fastest way to reach the guest house before Pete.

***

Spyker had been chatting with his girlfriend, Linda, on the phone. The girl was becoming torn in his flesh. She wanted to know where he was so she could come there. Spyker did not want to tell her that he was in Kinsama City. That would spell doom for him. He knew that Linda was a jealous girl, and she would believe that he went to Kinsama without her to have fun. As he was chatting with Linda, he saw the gateman open the gate of the bungalow, and in a minute, a Toyota Prado SUV entered the house. He picked up his phone and dialled Gudy's number. Gudy picked up the call at once. He described in a second all that he had seen. Gudy simply told him to be more vigilant and call him back if he noticed any other thing. From Spyker's description, he knew that Darrel did not lie to him, and Edyta was the owner of the house. He lit his Cuban cigar and waited for Spyker's call.

In his usual way, Pete said, "That's a lovely phone you have. Can I have a look?"

"No problem."

She gave him the iPhone 10.

Admiring the phone, Pete asked her the cost of the phone.

"Believe me! I don't know, and I don't care to know. That phone was given to me by my ex-boyfriend."

Pete exclaimed, "Your ex must be rich to give you this machine."

"He is, but we are no longer on good terms."

"Sorry about that; we, men, don't know what we have until we lose it. If I had such a beautiful lady as my girlfriend, I would have been the happiest man on the planet."

As he was close to the gate of the guest house, he blasted the horn of the car, and immediately the gate was opened. He parked the car in the parking lot and killed the sound.

"Here we are, Cendy. I hope you enjoyed my driving."

As he was talking, he carefully switched off the phone.

"You can say that again. What could I have done without you? Is this Sharon's house?" she asked.

"Yes, and I believe she is inside. Let's go in and surprise her."

***

Spyker's instinct never deceived him; he had reported to Gudy about a lady entering the house. All Gudy could tell him was to be vigilant. Seeing this tall, elegant girl entering the house meant one thing. And he believed that it was going to be a busy day for him. As he was watching closely at the bungalow, he saw a Toyota Avalon car approaching the gate of the bungalow. The gate opened at once, and a man and a lady came out of the car. He watched them enter the house and then called Gudy.

***

Cendy, moving in high spirits, entered the living room of the house, and a man and a lady greeted her.

She turned back to Pete, who was standing at her back and asked, "Where is Sharon?"

Without wasting time, Pete hit her on the neck, and she fainted.

Sharon dialled the number, but there was no response. She redialled it, and it said switched off.

She was confused and thought what the cause might be. Did she have a low battery? She ran back to her cab and asked him to take her to her house. As she entered the cab, she said a short prayer and closed the door of the car.

Tony and his boss sat at the corner of the bar, talking in low voices. Tony told Tim what Jordyn told him about Edyta. Tim was interested in the story. He told Tony to stick with Jordyn and not let him know that he was being followed.

"This might be the break we are waiting for, and I don't want you to mess it up. You might need a gun; come to my house in the evening, and I will give you one."

Giving him some naira notes for his expenses, he left.

Tony dialled Jordyn's number, and they talked for about 20 seconds before he cut the call.

Edyta's guest house was located on the outskirts of the town. It was one of the best architectural masterpieces in the area. It had two well-furnished living rooms, four bedrooms, and a well-equipped modern kitchen. The design of the building used all contemporary acrostic materials. When any of their victims were brought, no sound of crying could be heard outside by other people living within the neighbourhood.

"Where did you pick her up?" Edyta asked Pete.

"At the airport, and let me surprise you that she is a guest to the one and only Sharon, the media lady."

"Oh my God! You are kidding me! How did you know?"

"She told me herself."

In the past, Edyta and Sharon had a hard issue. One day, Edyta saw Sharon in one of the famous restaurants in the city and liked her. He approached and greeted her and introduced himself to Sharon. Sharon looked at Edyta from head to toe and left the place without a word. Nobody ever did that to Edyta before, and since then, Edyta had been looking for a way to get back at Sharon for disgracing him in such a manner. He thanked Pete for the job well done, opened his briefcase, produced a bundle of 1000 naira notes and gave them to Pete.

"Go and park the Avalon at the garage, disguise yourself a little bit, go to the city, and have both your eyes and ears to the ground; when I need you, I will call you."

He thanked his boss and did as he was instructed. He already had a plan on what to do. There was a new catch which he wanted to take out for dinner. All he needed to do was dash to his apartment to change his clothes, put on something casual, and call his new girlfriend.

On reaching her apartment, Sharon got out of the cab, paid her cabman off and opened her door. She went straight to her bar, found a bottle of gin, poured it into a glass cup, and drank the whole of it.

She sat down. Many things were coming to her mind. What would she do? She was pretty sure that Cendy was inside the plane. Would she call Cendy's parents to let them know what was happening? By then, the effect of gin had calmed her nerves a little bit. She decided to wait for another 30 minutes to see if her number was still off. As she had no option, she could either call Cendy's dad or go to the police.

When Cendy regained her consciousness, she found herself lying on the floor with blood coming out of her nose. Her legs and hands were tied together. She tried to cry, but her voice could not produce any sound. In the process, the door opened, and Edyta walked in with Lucy behind him. He said in a low voice, "Cendy, I guess that is your name, and you are a guest to Sharon, the media queen. Welcome to my abode."

"What do you want from me?" Cendy shouted to Edyta. Lucy moved forward and slapped her so hard. "If you don't keep quiet, I will hit you even harder. You have to listen and answer his questions."

Edyta continued, "My pretty lady, that's not the way to treat our special guest. However, let's go down to business. I'm a busy man, and I hate to repeat myself; all I want from you is that when I ask a question, you give me the correct answer and don't waste my time."

Cendy heard about kidnapping, and she had read about it, but little did she know in her life that she would be a victim?

As she looked at these captors of hers, hatred and agony filled her stomach as she had already started developing a soft spot for Pete, her kidnapper. She cried slowly.

Edyta put a hand inside his suit, pulled out Cendy's iPhone 10, and asked her for the security code. He searched for Sharon's name, found it and showed it to Cendy.

"Is it your friends' number?"

She nodded.

Edyta sat down on the corner of the bed and dialled Sharon's number.

***

Tony came back to the house and met his friend, Jordyn, in high spirits, who was working and putting some finishing touches on his paintings. He planned to work overnight to have something to show Edyta the next day before his business partners came. He planned to call him the next day to show him some of his best works.

As Tony entered the room, he greeted Jordyn.

"My brother, how far? You are looking so happy; what is the secret?"

"Tony, you know everything now; very soon, I will leave you in this God-forsaken room and find myself a bigger apartment. By the time I'm done with my exhibition, the money will come, and I'm pretty sure that none of Edyta's business partners will resist my paintings when they set their eyes on them."

"Let us get the money first and let it enter your big skull that if you get an apartment, I'm moving in with you."

"Not at all."

"Okay, let's get to the bridge first before we cross it."

Sitting by the corner of the bed, Tony looked at Jordyn and shook his head.

As Sharon was contemplating what to do, her phone rang. She picked up at once and saw that it was Cendy calling her. She connected the call and screamed, "Cendy, where are you? You have given me a heart attack."

The other end simply said, "Your friend is keeping us company. In your interest and the interest of your friend, don't call the police. My boys are watching your every move. Any mistake and Cendy will die. Wait for further instructions."

Edyta turned off the phone.

Sharon could not believe her ears, and as she wanted to walk out of the room, her legs were becoming too weak to carry her body, and she fainted.

***

Jordyn put the finishing touches on his paintings and was satisfied with his portfolio. To his amazement, he remembered that he had not eaten since morning. He stood up, went into the kitchen, opened the fridge and came out with canned food. He opened it and poured it onto a ceramic plate, timed the microwave for two minutes, placed the food inside, turned it on and waited. After eating, he lay on the bed, thinking about how he would see Edyta the next day. Within a couple of minutes, he dosed off. As Tony entered the room using a spare key, he saw his friend snoring. He moved slowly, in order not to wake him up. Tony went to Jordyn's briefcase, containing all his painting works. Jordyn always took the briefcase wherever he went. Tony opened it professionally and planted microchips in the bag. He tested it and found out that it is working. He placed the bag exactly where he had found it and went to the kitchen. He came back with a bottle of soft drink, sat down, and switched on the TV. His mind was preoccupied with what his boss, Tim. told him: "Stick with Jordyn and, please, don't mess up this time."

He knew that Tim had not forgiven him for one famous kidnapping case they handled at one particular time. He was still new in the business of Policing. He remembered that Tim, who was still a junior officer, had expected Tony to carry out simple instructions. He was asked to watch over the house of their target, but along the line, he was so uncomfortable because his bladder was heavy with urine. As he stepped out to ease himself, he failed to notice the suspect tip toying out of the house. He shook his head. He knew that he had built a lot of experience and confidence in this police job. He promised himself that he would never mess up this one. He lay down on the bed and slept off.

***

It was 1:40 pm, and Sharon had been in a coma for over an hour. She woke up looking at the time and thought she was dreaming, but she knew that this was for real. She stood up and sat on the sofa. What might be the condition of her friend, Cendy? She could not help but cry slowly.

She raised her phone to make a call, but she remembered that she was warned not to call anyone regarding this; otherwise, she would lose her friend. She thought of what to do, but her brain was empty. She needed to make calls, but what if her phone was being monitored. She remembered that there was a phone in the house she no longer used. She searched for the phone, saw it and switched on the phone. She was lucky that it was still okay. She quickly dialled a number.

***

"I saw the way you were looking at that girl. Let it not be what I'm thinking." Lucy was so empathetic about this issue as she knew Edyta very well. Edyta, who happened to be a womanizer, was preoccupied with what he saw on Cendy. Edyta loved what he saw as he was sitting on the sofa with a bottle of brandy – thinking of what to do. He did not want money from this lady but to make sure that Sharon paid dearly for disgracing him in public. But right inside his mind, he knew that this girl in his house was innocent and felt pity for her. He wished if he had Sharon as the hostage. He stood up, took a sip of the brandy and asked Lucy to go to the kitchen and prepare food for their visitor.

"Take care of the house; don't open the door for anybody, even if he is Pete. Let me go to town and put my ear on the ground."

Edyta moved out of the house holding the key of his latest Honda Accord car. He went straight to his garage, opened the car door and went inside it. He beckoned to the gateman to open the gate for him and warned him not to open the gate to anybody, and he drove off. Spyker saw him leave the house without the former car he came in with, and he redialled Gudy's number at once.

With much cash with him, Pete went straight to his one-room apartment and changed into something nice. He stepped inside his car with only one thing in mind — to pick his new girlfriend. As he was getting close to his girlfriend's house, he called her and asked her to be ready, as he was already close. Without wasting time, she put on her evening wear and went to the gate to wait for him.

***

Kentus was handsome and intelligent young man whose main job was to provide security to tourists who visited Kinsama town. He was a heavily built, athletic, and trained boxer. Because of the nature of his job, he had a license to carry a light weapon. Growing up in the village, he was once a hunter. He developed a special skill of using his local gun on wild animals. Growing up was not easy for Kentus. The story has it that he came to the city to find a job as a gateman, but luck smiled on him when one European saw him, liked him, and employed him as his bodyguard. He had been working with the man for over one year. It was through this benefactor that he was able to train as a boxer and learn the use of shotguns.

Last week was like a dream come true. He made a lot of money from the service he provided to some wealthy tourists and now, he wanted to give himself a special treatment. There was this Chinese restaurant in town he wanted to go to and have a good meal. As he locked his door, his phone rang. He picked up the phone, and it was Sharon at the other end, talking in a low tone, "This is Sharon, I'm in trouble, and I need to see you as soon as possible. And I believe I'm being watched."

"Sharon, calm down, find a way and meet me at Eddy's bar."

He put off the phone. Thinking of what might have made Sharon feel she was in trouble and being watched made him shiver a little bit. He went back to his apartment, got his shotgun, entered his car, and drove off to Eddy's bar.

It was 9.45 pm, and two men and a lady were speaking in a low tone while sitting in the corner of Eddy's bar. They had been there for close to two hours. Holding an expensive Cuba cigar in his left finger, Gudy took the cigar and breathed out expensive smoke from his nostrils. He took a sip of his drink to relax a little bit, looked around the environment, cleared his throat and said, "Trench, my friend, you may be wondering why I invited you to come over to Kinsama City. I have been in this city for two weeks now. I met this lady here the very first day I came in. She has been so helpful. Her name is Darrel. Let me refresh your memory. Two years ago, back in the Contuoo region, there was one man we entrusted our lives to within our drug business. We believed so much in this man that all the millions of dollars we had made were kept in his custody. It was agreed that we would share the money once the eyes of the government were off the case. However, a month before the agreed date of sharing the money, the trusted guy fled with the money. To cap it all, Don and other colleagues lost their lives when some of us believed that they had a hand in the disappearance of the money."

"My friend, Gudy, why are you telling me all this? I thought we had forgotten about this incident. Going back to this old story will not do us any good; rather, it will intensify our pain and agony."

"Relax, my friend," said Gudy, "I have a surprise for you. The architect of the whole thing has been living here since he left Contuoo. I hope you remember what I said. If you can recall, I told you, my trusted friend, I will have no rest or peace until I find Edyta. And to surprise you, Edyta lives in this big city."

"Holy Moses!" Trench stood up, went to Gudy, kissed him on the head, went to his seat and said, "Tell me more."

"He is living like a king here. He has a small office inside the city with one secretary, Darrel, who happens to be his girl. The office is just a smokescreen to cover his dubious business. He used our money to invest in hotels and other lucrative businesses in this town. But as the saying goes, once a crook, always a crook. He still indulges in drugs and kidnapping. So, my friend, I invited you here for us to visit Edyta."

Looking at Trench, Gudy smoked his cigar and he looked like a deadly killer.

"Oh my God! How did you come to know all this information?" Trench asked, drinking his beer. He stood up to adjust his belt. He took a sip of his beer as his hands shook. He tried to control it as Gudy watched him closely. He knew that when Trench was in this mood, what came into his mind was to kill. Trench was known among his colleagues as a ruthless killer of the group. Hot adrenaline rushed into his system, and he wished he had a gun then. Edyta, as the target, would just make his day.

"Sit down, my friend," Gudy said, "Let me introduce the lady in our midst. Meet Darrel, Edyta's secretary. As I told you earlier, I met her the first day I came to this town. I have been on Edyta's trace for some time now. I know he has been living in this town. So, when I met Darrel, one thing led to another. When I told her I came to this town in search of an old friend, little did I know that right in front of me was all I needed to know about Edyta, our friend?"

Trench sat down, and all that had happened in the Contuoo region came back to him in a flash; he remembered all the incidents as if they were yesterday. He was speechless, looked at Darrel, and asked his friend if the girl could be trusted.

Gudy answered, "Yes, my friend."

***

Edyta pulled over his Honda car in the parking lot of a tourist hotel, where he knew Sharon always hung around in the evening. On several occasions, he had sighted her relaxing in the poolside. He went straight to Chizy who had been working with him as a pimp. She also gave him information about the rich tourists in town who happened to lodge in their hotel. He saw Chizy serving one customer. He paused, moved over to one empty seat, and sat down. Having seen Edyta, Chizy rushed her service with her customer and went to him.

***

Sharon pulled herself together, went to her wardrobe, and changed into some free wear as there was no time to look at her attire. She knew that her caller warned her to stay and wait for his call. From what she read and the information she had gathered, she knew that nobody might be watching her. But even at that, she had to be very careful. She picked up her two phones, unlocked the door leading to a corridor and knocked at the door of her co-tenant. The door opened at once. Emmy was surprised to see Sharon jumping into his apartment. Sharon told him that one of his clients was in town and had invited her to Eddy's bar, but her Motor was in the garage with the mechanic. So she would be happy if he could find the time to take her there. Emmy went into his bedroom, came back with his car key, and locked his apartment up. As he reached the garage, he unlocked the car and opened the door for Sharon and they drove out of the gate.

Sharon was looking through her shoulder to know whether they were being followed or not. Satisfied that they had no company, she relaxed a bit. Emmy knew Sharon very well; they had been living as co-tenants for over four years, but he had never seen Sharon look so terrified. He wanted to ask her if all was well with her, but knowing Sharon, he assumed she would not tell him much. He decided to mind his own business. Within a couple of minutes, they arrived at Eddy's bar. Sharon thanked him and moved out of the car. Emmy reversed the car, waited a little bit and drove off.

She quickly moved towards Eddy's bar. Every now and then, she looked over her shoulder to see if she was being followed. As she was coming close to Eddy's bar, she saw two men and a lady leaving the bar. She had never seen them before, but little did she know that the lady knew her too well? Darrel had been a fan of Sharon. She never knew Sharon as somebody who kept late at night. She looked through her shoulder and saw how fast she was walking. At that moment, she knew all was not well with Sharon.

"Chizy, my sweetheart, how have you been? Long time no see!" said Edyta.

"Stop flattering me; I know you no longer need my services. I wonder who the new person is. At least, for old time's sake, once in a while, come around, for I still have eyes on what you need, and believe me, you have been missing a lot."

"Chizy, you know me very well."

He dipped inside his pocket, brought out some naira notes, and gave them to her.

"This money is for you. I have missed your company for quite some time now. Tell me! Have you seen Sharon lately?"

"Of course, she was here in the morning to catch up with some tourists. She didn't stay long but came back between 11 am and 12 noon; I'm not sure of the time."

"Do you know why she came back?"

"Yes, she forgot her phone; she was charging her phone but forgot to plug it out, so she came back looking for it. It's the storekeeper who gave it to her. One thing I noticed was that she was not herself."

"What do you mean by she was not herself?"

"I know Sharon for some time now. She is somebody who carries herself like a queen, but seeing her that afternoon tells me one thing. All is not well with her."

Edyta talked for a few seconds and told her that he would be coming in two days to see her. Chizy thanked him for the money and left. Edyta looked up and down and saw a lady drinking beer all alone. He wanted to go and toast her, but knowing that he had a lot at stake, he picked up his car key and left the hotel. He needed to know what Lucy and their visitor had been doing.

***

On reaching Eddy's bar, Kentus parked his car in the parking lot and went to the corner of the swimming pool, his favourite area. He liked the place for one reason. The location was always a little bit dark, and he could see any visitor coming to the swimming pool without the person seeing him. He requested a glass of Brandy. A lady came with his request, greeted him and left. In his mind, he had been thinking of Sharon. Why did she have to call her with such fear in her voice? He knew Sharon as a strong woman. What might have happened to her? Was she in danger, as she said? He went down, touched his gun holder, and was satisfied that it was still there. His confidence came back to him. He sipped his Brandy and lit his cigarette. He looked at his watch, was worried, and soliloquized, "I shouldn't have asked her to come to Eddy's bar. What if she is really in trouble? The distance between her house and Eddy's bar is less than 20 minutes. I have to go and look for her." As he stood up, he saw somebody coming towards his direction. He looked closely and saw that it was Sharon. He sat back and relaxed.

Sharon came straight to him and greeted him. He responded and offered her a cigarette, which she refused.

"My pretty lady, what is eating you up?" Kentus asked.

Sharon narrated all that happened, from when her tyre disappointed her on her way to the airport to when she received a call from a man who claimed he had kidnapped Cendy. As she finished her story, she was highly exhausted, sweating like a Christmas goat about to be slaughtered. Kentus stretched his hand and held her.

"My friend, take it easy; it's going to be okay. It's certain that your friend has been kidnapped. Have you informed the police?"

"Not yet," Sharon answered, crying bitterly and wiping her face with her handkerchief.

"Would you like to stay with me, or do you want me to take you back to your apartment?"

"Take me to my apartment."

"Good, let's go."

Kentus led the way to where he parked his car. He entered, opened the door for Sharon, and sped up the vehicle.

"Wait for my call tomorrow morning. Don't call the police yet. Let me go to the city and ask some questions," Kentus said.

Sharon simply said, "Get my friend back for me."

In less than 20 minutes, Kentus pulled over at the back of Sharon's apartment like a ghost, walked to her house door, opened it and entered. Watching her from his car, Kentus knew that he was going to have a busy night. He drove off to the uptown bar. There was a man Kentus helped in the past. His name was Randy. Randy was a crook. He went to jail every now and then. One day, he and his gang were robbing a grocery shop, but little did they know that the police were around the corner? Some passersby who noticed what was happening in the shop alerted the police at once. Others were lucky, but not Randy, as he was shot in the hand by the police but still escaped with the wound. On that fateful day, Kentus was around the corner, watching what was happening. He saw where Randy hid but did not alert the police. When the police searched him everywhere but could not find him, they left. He took Randy to his house and treated him for his gun wound. Within two weeks, Randy got healed, and Kentus advised him to stay out of the robbery. After that, Kentus let him go. Since then, Randy has been working for Kentus, especially in intelligent gathering with regard to activities of the underworld. He knew that once he could reach Randy, he would know at once who was behind this kidnap. Without wasting time, he increased the speed of his car to the uptown bar where he knew Randy always stayed. On getting to the uptown bar, he saw Randy playing snooker with his friends; he allowed him to finish his game. He went to the corner of the bar and requested for a bottle of beer. Randy spotted the last snooker ball on the hole and was celebrating his victory with his cigarette when he looked at the corner of the bar and saw his friend taking his beer with a stick of cigar in his hand. He knew at once that Kentus being there was not a coincidence; rather, he was there in search of information. He left his friends and went to meet him. Kentus greeted him and asked him to sit down. He beckoned to the barman for another cup of beer for his friend. Randy took the first cup of beer as if his life depended on it. He requested another cup. Kentus sipped, cleared his throat and said to his friend, "Long time no see. What has been going on in Kinsama city?"

Randy simply said, "A lot, my friend. It depends on the area you want to know."

"Tell me honestly all you know about Edyta's recent activities."

Randy looked at his friend with keen interest and said, "I saw his boy Pete this evening. You know, for some time now, Edyta and his boys have been laying low because the police are in their tracks. Pete confirmed to me that they are back in business."

Randy paused for a moment and looked at his beer cup, which was already empty. As Randy looked at Kentus, Kentus knew what that meant. He called the barman and requested another cup of beer. Randy nodded his thanks and continued. In a low tone, he said, "This morning, they have a beautiful damsel in their nest."

Kentus blew thick, expensive smoke out of his nostrils. He was calm; he did not want Randy to know that the information he had just dropped meant a lot to him. In his mind, he was thinking of what to do. Whether to call the police and alert them or not was his contemplation. It was too early to tell the police. Besides, he still needed to confirm the story before informing the police. He knew Edyta very well. He knew that he was a very intelligent crook. He was aware of where he kept his victim. He was tempted to ask Randy further questions but decided not to. He simply asked Randy for any news about their drug business, and Randy had no story on that. Kentus thanked him for his time, opened his wallet and gave Randy some naira notes. Randy thanked him. Kentus looked at his wristwatch, and it was some minutes into the early morning. He paid the barman and stood up as he had only one thing in mind: to confirm the story Randy had just told him and be sure that the victim was Sharon's friend. He went into his car and drove off to Boulevard Street. He drove past Edyta's gate, hid the car in the corner of the street, came out, and tiptoed towards the edge of Edyta's gate. As he was inspecting the wall to see if he could climb it, he saw the headlights of a car at a distance. He immediately hid in flowers around the fence. The vehicle came to Edyta's gate and stopped. From where he was hiding, he could see the person inside the car and know at once that it was Edyta. The gateman opened the gate, and as soon as Edyta drove inside, the gate was closed. Kentus came out of his hiding place, found one tree near the fence, and climbed it. He saw Edyta coming out of his car with a bottle of Brandy in his hand. The front entrance door opened, and he saw a lady come out of the building and greet Edyta.

"Where have you been?" the lady asked.

"Did the lady give you any problem?"

"Not really, but I was worried."

They were talking in such a low tone that Kentus was finding it difficult to hear what Edyta was saying, but he heard something that sounded like Sharon. He tried to press his ear harder but could not hear anything. As two people entered the house and locked the door, he climbed down. At least he knew that what Randy told him was correct and that the girl Edyta kidnapped must be Sharon's friend. He went to where he hid his car, entered and drove off. When all this drama was going on,

Spyker was busy with infrared binoculars watching Kentus from the time he hid his car to when he climbed down from the tree. He even watched Edyta drive to enter the house. He simply called Gudy, but since he was asleep, he picked up after some time. Spyker told him all he watched. Gudy was pleased, thanked him and asked him to be more vigilant. He switched off the phone.

It was 7 am when Jordyn woke up in high spirits. He went to the kitchen and made an omelette with a cup of tea and a slice of bread. He quietly took his breakfast, went to his cubicle, took out his briefcase, and packed all the paintings he wanted to show to Edyta in it. With satisfaction, he locked the briefcase, went to the bathroom and took a quick shower. He could not hold back his joy as he remembered what Edyta had told him about his business partners. He smiled and started whistling the melodious song of Majek Fashek – 'Send down the rain'. He came out of the bathroom and went to his wardrobe to select a dark-coloured suit with a nice tie. Within a couple of minutes, he was ready to go to Edyta's office. Back in the bedroom, Tony was pretending to be sleeping. He had been watching his friend Jordyn with much enthusiasm, and he knew that all this excitement from Jordyn was because his friend believed that Edyta would attend to his single ambition of organizing an exhibition for his paintings. Before Jordyn woke up, he had already had his bath but went back to bed and pretended to be sleeping. Jordyn came into the room, touched Tony on the back, and Tony raised his head.

"Good morning, Mr. T. I'm good to go."

"Woo! You are up already."

"Yes, my friend, I want to be the first person Edyta will see in his office today."

"Are you too sure of this, your guy, Edyta?"

"You will not understand, my friend."

Tony wished him good luck, and he left.

As soon as he closed the door, Tony jumped out of bed and dressed up within two minutes. He locked their door, ran out of the street and saw his friend walking majestically towards the bus stop. Tony allowed him to enter the cab, quickly ran to the bus stop, and asked the cabman to follow him. Inside the cab, he activated the chip he planted in Jordyn's briefcase. As Tony selected the frequency from his Android phone, he put on the earphone and could hear Jordyn discussing with his cabman. Satisfied and relaxed, he had to maintain a five-hundred-meter radius so as not to lose reception. He asked his driver to maintain the same speed as Jordyn's cab. Jordyn's cab pulled over in front of Edyta's office in less than 12 minutes. He paid the man, carried his briefcase, jumped out of the car, and opened the front door leading to the staircase. He mounted the stairs and looked at his wristwatch; it was 8:39 am. He wondered if the secretary had come. He said a short prayer and wished himself good luck. Tony paid off his cabman to maintain his reception range with Jordyn. He had never been to Edyta's office before, but as he opened the front door, he saw the staircase and carefully followed it, moving slowly. On getting to the staircase landing, he saw two doors. Looking closer, he saw Edyta's name written boldly on one of the doors. The second door had the sign of cybercafé, and he quickly entered. A young lady aged between 19 and 21 came and greeted him. Tony cleverly asked her if their internet was working and that he wanted to make use of their computer. The lady said yes, and he requested that he be given one hour of airtime. The lady went inside a smaller office, came out with a small piece of paper and gave it to him. He gave her some money and asked her to keep the change. Tony sat down, logged on to the computer, and pretended to be working. It was time to hear Jordyn discussing with Edyta's secretary through his earphone.

"He called this morning to inform me that he might not be coming to the office today because he was not feeling fine." She could see the disappointment on Jordyn's face. Out of pity, she asked Jordyn if she had his boss's phone number. Jordyn said, "No." She opened her drawer, brought out Edyta's complementary card and gave it to him. Jordyn thanked her and left the office in anger. Tony horridly logged off the computer and left. He dialled Tim's number and told him his next line of action. After thinking for a while, Tim approved it and asked Tony to be careful.

***

Trench, after he met with Gudy, went back to his hotel room. The two men had agreed to meet at 8 am. He took off his jacket and went to the bathroom to take his bath. He mixed a strong drink of Brandy, lay on his bed, and went through all his friend Gudy had told him about Edyta. He thought Gudy was joking back in the Contuoo region when he said that he would track down Edyta even if it took his life. He remembered how Don lost his life and how Edyta fled with their money. Goosebumps filled his body. His business had not been doing well for some time now. He saw this as a big break he had been praying for. If he and Gudy laid a hand on that money Edyta took from the group, he would come back to life again, reconcile with the girl of his dreams, and take her for shopping in Paris. His only disappointment was that he did not come prepared. He should have come with his favourite gun. But as much as he did not prepare for this, he knew quite well that Gudy was well-prepared, and he had so much trust in him. After rolling and rolling in the bed, he finally slept off and woke up around 6.30 am to call the restaurant for his breakfast. He went into the bathroom, cleaned himself up, and came out. The waiter was ready with his order. He paid her, lit his cigarette, and started eating his breakfast. He went to the bedside telephone and dialled the receptionist's number. A lady picked at once.

"Connect me to room 313," he said.

"In a minute, sir," said the receptionist.

In a couple of seconds, Gudy's voice came live in the phone speaker. "Trench, how are you doing?" asked Gudy.

"I'm cool," Trench replied.

"You can come over to my room if set."

"I'm set, bro."

"Then come over at once because we have a lot to talk about."

Trench finished his cigarette, picked up his mobile phone and left his room.

***

Kentus, sitting on his bed, was highly worried. He did not know what to do. The realization that Edyta was holding Sharon's girlfriend hostage baffled him. He remembered that he promised to call Sharon in the morning. He dialled Sharon and told her to be calm and that sooner or later, he would be calling her to give her useful information. He told Sharon not to call the police yet until he said so. He hung up. He only knew Edyta, but they had not met before. Randy had told him much about Edyta; he knew that he was a ruthless crook who indulged in all kinds of crime. But what baffled him was that the police had never caught him. He had to figure out how to visit him in the house to rescue Cendy. He had to find out how many people were there in that bungalow. He had seen Edyta, a lady, and his gateman when he climbed the tree. The way he saw the gateman, he did not appear to him as a fighter. He could take care of him without a problem. He paused, trying to remember if he had seen a dog or heard the voice of one. But he was not too sure if he had heard or seen anything that looked like a dog. He had to be sure; he had to go there that night, look around, and come up with a plan for how to visit him. Right inside his heart, he knew he could rescue Cendy without much problem if he planned it well. He was optimistic that he could do it. So, he went ahead and prepared his strategy.

***

On getting back to the house, Jordyn found Tony relaxing on the bed and going through some documents. Tony greeted him and asked him how his meeting with Edyta went. Jordyn was not happy, but he managed to tell him what the secretary had said to him, that Edyta was not feeling well. But the only good thing about it was that she gave him his complimentary card so that he could call him.

Tony said, "Why not call him at once? You might not know; he may even invite you to his house; don't you think so?"

"Okay, let me try him then."

Jordyn picked up his mobile phone and dialled Edyta's number; it was ringing, but there was no answer. He tried again, and after some attempts, he finally answered. Edyta's voice simply said, "Who is this?"

Jordyn told him who he was and that he had gone to the office to show him the paintings, but the secretary said to him that he was not feeling okay.

"I'm so sorry," said Edyta, "Are you with the pictures, or did you drop them off with my secretary?"

"I'm with them, sir."

"Okay, you should have dropped them with her so whenever I come around, I can have a look at them and give you a call."

Jordyn was excited.

"That's not a problem; I can go back and drop them with her, sir."

"Then do that as soon as possible."

The phone went off.

Jordyn horridly explained his discussion with Edyta to Tony and left. Tony was so happy because he knew that sooner or later, Edyta would pick up the briefcase, and he would be monitoring all his discussions. He called his boss, Tim, and educated him on the latest happenings. Tim was excited and asked him to pick up a car and come at once to his apartment.

"Only I think you need a car to follow the briefcase."

Tony rushed out of the house, jumped into a cab, and went straight to Tim's house.

***

Gudy, as usual, was smoking his cigar when Trench entered his room. He stood up, went to his bathroom, and came back without the cigar. He sat down, faced Trench and asked him, "Are you in or out?"

Trench had been expecting this question from Gudy. He knew Gudy very well. He was a man who would always allow you to make your decision without any prejudice.

"Gudy, you know that I'm in."

"Good, let's go down to business."

"You know, just as I do, that Edyta is a brilliant and intelligent man. And we have to handle him well before he can cough out something from the money he took from us. As I told you earlier, I employed Spyker, who has been monitoring the building around the clock."

He reached for his Galaxy phone and showed Trench the pictures of Edyta's building he had taken.

"You can see from the pictures that there are only two buildings in the compound, the main building and the gateman's house. According to the information I received from Spyker, the only people in the building are two ladies. The first one normally comes out, but since the second one entered, she has not come out of the building. He has a gateman but no dog. Within the building, there is a tree that one can easily climb and enter the compound. What bothers me is that last night, Spyker reported to me that there was one young man who was spying on Edyta. He saw the man climb one of the trees around midnight. He was not sure if he was a policeman or not, but it's my guess he was not a police. Even if he is a police, we will take care of him if he becomes a problem, or do you have a counter view?"

"No, my friend."

"This is my plan; I would like us to hit this night. By 7 pm, we will relocate to Spyker's apartment. All we need to carry out the job is there. As soon as Edyta leaves the building, we will snick into the compound using one of the trees or through the back fence; we will get hold of the gateman and wait for Edyta to come back. When he comes back, we will open the gate for him and make him lead us inside his bungalow. Once inside, we will discuss with him the terms on which he will release the money to us. On getting the money, we may make away with his life because he has given us a lot of pain. He has to pay dearly for the life of Don and other members of our group who had lost their lives in the course of recovering this money."

Trench was only listening and nodding his head as Gudy was going through his plan.

"I know getting the money is not going to be easy, but I'm sure once we apply good intelligence, he will play along. This may last two or three days, but all I know is that I'm not leaving that house without my money. So, my friend, this is how I think we will handle it."

Trench only nodded to show his approval. He knew that Gudy was ever ready for this operation. For him, as much as Gudy was ready, there was no course for alarm. As far as he knew Gudy, he had never failed. He masterminded the release of one of their hitmen back in the Contuoo region, who was in police custody. Most of the people within the circle did not believe him, but to everyone's amazement, he, with their team, came out with the hitman. After that, he became the leader of the group.

"That's okay by me," Trench said at last.

***

Jordyn, carrying his briefcase, went outside. This time around, there was no need to go to the bus stop. Luckily, he got a cab right in front of their apartment. He checked his wallet, and there were some naira notes there. He counted and was satisfied that it could take care of his transport fare. It did not take long before a cab came. Without much discussion, he jumped inside the cab and directed the cab driver to take him to Edyta's office. Tony, watching from the balcony, moved like a Leopard into the garage, where he hid the car Tim gave him and followed Jordyn's cab. On reaching Edyta's office, Jordyn entered the office. After his discussion with the secretary, she collected the briefcase and bade him goodbye. Tony was in his usual place, pretending to be working on the computer. He heard all the discussion of Jordyn and Darrel and told himself that he would be going to stay longer in the cafe. He requested for a bottle of Coca-Cola and a meat pie. He knew that Jordyn had gone. He believed that sooner or later, Edyta would come for the paintings. He relaxed, logged on to the computer, went to his favourite websites and started downloading the contents. Within two hours, he heard Edyta greeting his secretary. He overheard him asking his secretary if he had a message from someone. The secretary simply said yes, reached where she kept the briefcase and handed it over to Edyta. She carefully looked at her boss and imagined all Gudy had been telling her about him. She knew that the man in front of him was a liar and deceitful. Even though she knew that Gudy was a terrible guy, she trusted him more than her so-called boss. She wanted to find out if all she had heard from Gudy was true. She went to Edyta, held his hand, adjusted his tie, and said, "I'm missing you; you hardly have my time these days."

Edyta looked at her gently, pushed her, collected his car key and asked her to take care of the office. Darrel, pretending to be at ease, went to where her seat was, sat down and slowly said to Edyta, "Most of you do drugs."

Edyta could not believe what he was hearing from his secretary. He loved Darrel so much that he had been nursing the idea of proposing marriage to her. The shock was like cold water splashing all over his body. He recovered from the shock, went to Darrel and said to her, "What did you just say?"

Darrel saw the look on his face. Fearing that he might harm her, she said, "It's everywhere. Why do you have to do drug business? So all this while you have been lying to me?"

Edyta could not believe his ears. He simply said to Darrel, "I don't understand what you are talking about. I have warned you to stay out of gossipers."

He moved close to Darrel and raised his hand to beat her but dropped it. "Not only that you do drugs but you kidnap too.

Who knows who you have kidnapped now that made you relocate to Boulevard Street?"

As she dropped the word, Edyta felt like the earth would open and swallow him. Darrel was watching her boss and lover's reaction and knew immediately that Gudy was right. Edyta, in a state of helplessness, shouted at her and said, "Who has been talking to you? Who has been feeding you with all these lies about me?"

Darrel walked closer to him, held him by his shirt and told him, "You know I love you so much. You have been kind to me, and there is nothing I cannot do for you. I was at Eddy's bar last night with a couple of my friends. After a while, I decided to visit the ladies' room, and I overheard some group of men talking about you."

"It's all lies; you know I cannot do it. This is a plan of my enemies to bring me down." Edyta was shouting at the top of his voice. He could not control himself. Darrel was just watching him. Seeing her boss and the person she had loved so much, she simply went back to her seat, collected her handbag, went to Edyta, kissed him on the forehead and left. Edyta was standing in the middle of his office like a statue. He thought he was dreaming. In the corner of the office, the only noise was coming from the television. He went close to the TV to switch it off and overheard a popular pastor ministering on the TV, saying: "The wages of sin is death; repent and be saved." On hearing this, he switched off the television, picked up Jordyn's briefcase, locked his office and left. As he stepped out of the corridor, he saw Tony strolling down the staircase. He walked past Tony and greeted him, but Tony did not reply. If he had known that the man he just greeted had the keys that might lock him up in jail throughout his life, he should have looked at him twice to mark him as his enemy or, better still, kill him. Tony was watching Edyta as he walked past him. He had the urge to arrest him, but he knew he still needed to call Tim. As he stepped out, he went where he parked his car and drove off. He called Tim and said, "I have made an important discovery and would like to see you at once."

Tim simply said, "Come over to my office then."

He increased the speed of his car towards Tim's office.

Edyta's garage in the office was at the back of the building, and it took him three minutes to reach there. Inside his car, he felt like someone was following him. The feeling was so strong that he kept on looking over his shoulder. Darrel had said that a group of men were talking about him. Who were this group of men? He hardly discussed his business with anybody. The only person who knew a little bit about his business was Pete. Had Pete sold him out? He had known Pete for quite some time now, and both of them had pulled serious business together that changed Pete's life. He knew he would not do anything that would jeopardize his source of income.

He planned to get rid of Pete before the year ran off because he had known too much. But with the situation on the ground, if he did that now, he might blow his cover. He liked this city very much. Since he came to this city, he had been living in affluence. He was making cool money even though he came to the city with a lot of money from Contuoo. The thought of Gudy flashed in his mind like a dream. Could it be that Gudy had traced him to this town? His heartbeat was racing up. Whenever he was in this kind of situation, he always felt nasty pain in his heart. He had been taking medication for it, but it kept on appearing. He went to the pigeonhole of his car, opened it, and there was the drug he normally took whenever he felt like that. He took two tablets and returned it. He tried to relax, but this odd feeling that someone was watching him kept coming. The only group he was so afraid of was Gudy's and Trench's. But, in the last two months, he had engaged Jim to take care of them for him. He now remembered that since then, he had not called Jim. He quickly went to his phone to find Jim's number. He dialled it, and after some time, he picked.

"Jim, how are things going in the Contuoo region?"

"A lot has been happening."

"What about Gudy and Trench? I believe by now you have handled them."

"Not really! You know, those two boys are like a snake. I was on their trail, but all of a sudden, they disappeared without a trace. Just this morning, I learned from a reliable source that Trench is on vacation in the coastal town of Kinsama."

On hearing this, the phone fell from Edyta's hand. What was really happening? How did Trench get to know he was in Kinsama, or was it only a coincidence? He picked up his phone, managed to talk with Jim for a few seconds, and got off his phone. He, in his car, drove straight to Boulevard Street.

***

Tony went into his boss's office and saw Ann, his boss's secretary, going through a file. He went to the only empty chair in the office and sat down. "Get rid of all these files, take them to your office and sort them out. I will call you later," said Tim.

She collected the files, gave Tony a sexy look and left the office.

"Tony, tell me all about the discovery, I'm all ears," Tim said excitedly.

Without wasting time, Tony laid all the discussion between Edyta and her secretary on the table.

"The angle I don't understand is what her secretary meant when she told Edyta that he had relocated to Boulevard Street.

Does it mean that he has property on Boulevard Street? If he does, I believe a lot has been going on there," Tony said.

Tim thought for a moment and digested all Tony had told him. He knew this was the big break they had been waiting for. If they could pull this through, have something to hook on Edyta, and get him arrested sooner or later, he would be promoted along with his partner. He stood up, collected his car key and asked Tony to follow him.

"We have much work to do," said Tim.

The two men did not talk. A lot was going through in Tim's mind. What if what Edyta's secretary said was nothing but a false alarm? Even if it was a false alarm, he had nothing to lose. He had to do what he believed was right. Within some minutes, they were in the office of the land registry. Tim had been a good friend to James, the land registry of Kinsama, a position he had been holding for over seven years now. As Tim and Tony entered his office, he welcomed Tim and asked him what had brought him to his office that afternoon.

Tim said, "It's all about police work, my friend. I have someone I would like you to check for me to know if he owns a property on Boulevard Street."

"Is that all?" said James.

"Yes, for now, my friend," said Tim.

James reached for his laptop, logged on, and asked Tim the name of the person. Tim wrote the name of Edyta and gave it to him. James typed in the name given to him and waited.

"I have not seen you lately; you hardly come to the club these days. Actually, police work is keeping you busy," said James.

"James, you know everything; the new police chief has put me on my toes as he hardly decides anything without my contribution. I have been busy; even my woman has started complaining," Tim explained.

As they were discussing, James glanced at his laptop, and there was property registered in the name of Edyta Cook, No. 8 Boulevard Street. "That's all I can see here, my friend," said James.

Tim and Tony looked at each other. Tim stood up, thanked James, and told Tony it was time to go. They left the office and went straight to the car.

"The eagle has landed," Tim said to Tony, "You have to relocate to Boulevard Street for now. You must locate the building and then have a close monitor on the building round the clock. If you can do it alone, good; if not, I can assign one officer to you."

"No need to worry, boss; I can handle it."

They drove back to Tim's office. Tim told Tony all he needed to do and then wished him good luck. Tony entered his car and drove off. In his mind, the first thing he thought of doing was going to his apartment and relaxing a bit. Thinking of the best approach, he assured himself that the eagle had landed and it was time to remove its wing so it could not fly again. Jordyn was not in the house when he came in. He hurriedly changed his clothes to something more casual and free. He packed one or two things inside his bag and left. His job was to locate the building and plan the next line of action.

***

Edyta hurriedly entered his house and met Lucy in the living room but did not talk to her. He went to his bar, prepared a strong gin for himself and drank all of it at once. Lucy, discovering that his hand was shaking, went to him, held his hand, collected the glass cup from him, and made him sit down.

"What is the problem? You are looking so nasty. See how you are shaking."

Edyta opened his mouth to say something, but no word came out. He tried again, but still the same thing. Lucy held his two hands and asked him to relax.

"Prepare another drink for me, please," said Edyta.

Lucy went to the bar and made something stronger for him. Edyta took it at once. He looked at Lucy as the effect of the drink calmed his nerves down a little bit. He told Lucy all Darrel had told him and also his call to Jim. Lucy had never seen Edyta in this type of situation before. She found it too difficult to believe that Edyta, whom she saw as a role model, was behaving in this manner. Lucy reached for her handbag, brought out her cigarette and lit it. She threw the packet of the cigarette to Edyta, who picked it up and lit his own. Silently, both of them smoked the cigarette, and within a couple of minutes, the effect of the cigarette calmed his nerves further. He looked at Lucy as she breathed out thick smoke and said, "Get me a cup of water, please."

Lucy stood up, went to the kitchen, opened the refrigerator, poured chilled water into a glass cup and brought it to him. He took the glass cup of water, drank the whole of it at a stretch, and handed the empty glass cup back to Lucy.

Lucy simply asked, "Are you okay now?"

He nodded in agreement, stood up and went to the room where they kept Cendy.

Cendy saw him and started crying, "Please, allow me to go. Believe me; I will not tell anyone what happened; please, I beg you in whatever you believe in."

Edyta went to her, hit her so hard and asked her to keep quiet.

"By tomorrow, I will be calling Sharon for ransom; pray that she will afford what I will request from her. If not, consider yourself a dead person."

He left the room and came back to the living room, "I think, tonight, we will be getting rid of this lady. I will see Pete tonight to have a word with him and see if he has been opening his mouth so wide. When I come back, based on what I found out from him, we will decide what to do with this lady."

Lucy did not want to argue with him. She knew quite well that when he was in this kind of mood, it meant disaster. She went inside one of the rooms, collected her handbag, came into the living room and met Edyta there making a call. She listened carefully to know who he was calling. "Pete, I would like to see you this evening; it's essential," said Edyta.

On seeing Lucy with her handbag, he cut the call, went where she was standing, held her by her waist and drew her to himself. Lucy did not resist him. He looked into her eyes, and Lucy bent down her head and kissed him. Edyta kissed her back and whispered to her that he had missed her so much. Lucy did not say a word but held Edyta so hard that he was even finding it difficult to breathe. Edyta slowly unzipped her blouse, and it fell on the floor like a feather. He carried her to his bedroom, and within some minutes, both lovers were consumed in the passion of their intimacy. At that moment, he forgot the problem he was facing. He felt that he was in a world of his own, where there was no stress and pain.

Lucy being good in bed, loving Edyta, and intending to end up as his wife gave him the satisfaction of his life. She knew that Edyta was a womanizer, and she believed that if she could handle him sexually, he would be her forever. She gave her whole self to Edyta, and within some time, they were exhausted. Edyta rolled off her, feeling weak and tired, and did not say a word to her. His eyelids were becoming heavy. He wanted to fight it, but the more he tried, the more unbearable it became. Lucy noticed what was happening to Edyta and encouraged him to sleep by rubbing her hand on his back. Gradually, he surrendered to the superior call of nature and slept off. Lucy stood up, went to the bath, had a cold shower, dressed up, went to the kitchen, and started preparing dinner for her lover. She knew he would need good food once he woke up.

***

Spyker had seen Edyta going into the building and had reported to Gudy. Gudy told him that he would be coming down in the evening to relieve him of his duty. Spyker could not hide his joy. He wanted to leave this God-forsaken place and go back to his woman. He picked up his phone and called a flight agent to book his flight. He wanted to call his girlfriend but resisted the urge. He went to the room where his belongings were kept, brought out his bag and started packing his clothes and belongings. After completing the packing, he went to the kitchen. There was one drink he had been keeping there for a day like this. He brought out the drink from the freezer, opened it, poured out a full glass cup, drank it at once, poured another glass, and his phone rang. It was his girlfriend. He picked up the call and said, "Baby, good that you have called. I will be seeing you tomorrow, baby. Please, cook my best food for me; we have a lot to discuss."

She kissed her in the air and switched off the phone.

***

Tony, dressed in faded jeans and a cap to disguise himself, parked his car on the street adjacent to Boulevard Street. From there, he trekked down to Boulevard Street, looking both left and right and counting the numbers of the buildings.

After a while, he located No. 8 Boulevard. He saw the bungalow as he was a man with a photographic memory. He had captured every detail about the building: the tree, the flowers, and affirmed that he would be in this building that night. Fortunately, Spyker saw him walking lazily along the road. He watched Tony walk past his building, but since he did not consider him a threat, he disregarded him and went back to his drink. Tony went where he parked his car and drove off. Nowhere in mind, he went through his plan again and remembered that he needed torchlight. He drove to one of the convenience shops around the corner, parked his car and went inside. There were two men also in the shop picking what they wanted for the same operation. Both of them exchanged pleasantries with Tony. Gudy and Trench were just feeling relaxed, picking one or two things they might use in Edyta's house. Only if they had known that the man they just saw in the convenience shop was an undercover police officer and that they would be reencountering him that night, they would have looked at him twice or, better still, aborted the operation and fled the city. But the truth is that man is powerless to prevent a tragedy meant for him. Satisfied with all they had picked, they paid their bill and left the shop. They drove to no 7 Boulevard Street, where they met Spyker in a celebration mood. He greeted them and told them that he was only happy that he would be going home to meet with his woman the next day. Both Trench and Gudy exchanged a glance and laughed. Gudy came to him and handed over some naira notes to him.

"Spyker, I appreciate you. Once again, you have proven to me that you are still one of my best men, and I advise you to keep it up. You are free to go. My friend and I will continue where you stopped," said Gudy.

Spyker thanked him, went inside the room he used as a bed, a room he scarcely used, collected his bag, wished his boss good luck and left. There was one hotel that he had seen the advertisement on television. He loved the hotel and wanted to spend a night there. As he moved out of the building, he saw a taxi, stopped it, and told the driver the name of the hotel. The taxi man simply said, "Jump in, my friend," and drove off. Both men went through their plan once again. Trench was at ease with the plan. The only thing he was worried about was getting their money back from Edyta. Gudy promised him that he would not leave the house without the money. But the question was: Did he keep his money in his house? If not, it was going to be an uphill task to get the money from Edyta. He wanted to raise this topic to Gudy but decided to keep quiet. Gudy handed him over the binoculars and said, "Keep watching the house. I would like to have a quick nap."

He left, went straight into the bedroom, picked up his phone, and dialled Darrel. She picked up the phone and said, "I will not be in the hotel tonight. I have urgent business to attend to; I will see you tomorrow morning."

"Okay, dearly, I will be waiting," she said and cut off the call. After that, he lay on the bed with a cigar in his hand. He told himself that sooner or later, he would come face to face with Edyta and would ruthlessly deal with him. Within a short time, he slept off.

***

Kentus went to where he kept his 22 police automatic gun. Even though he was licensed to carry light weapons, he hardly used it. But then, he thought he might need it. He cleaned and oiled it and put it back in the gun holder. He already had a plan on what to do that night. All he knew was that he must come back alive with Cendy. He also knew that it was not going to be easy. He called Sharon and said, "Sharon, this is Kentus. If I don't call you by 12:30 am, please put a call through the number I will send you. Don't forget, please."

He hung up, and the time was 6:16 pm. He had a good dinner, which he ordered from a popular restaurant in town. It was his culture to eat very well whenever he had this type of job. After dinner, he took a glass of wine and then lit a cigarette. He remembered that he had not sent the phone number of his police friend to Sharon. He promised to send it earlier. He had somehow briefed his police friend that he had been working on a job and that someone might call him should anything go wrong. He planned to leave the house around 10 pm to Boulevard Street and smuggle himself into the building, and other things would follow.

***

It was 7:34 when Edyta woke up from his sleep. Both the pain in his heart and the fear in him had all gone. He went into the bathroom, took a quick shower, dressed up, and came into the living room. He saw Lucy busy watching television in the living room. He came to her, kissed her on the forehead and whispered *thank you* in her ears. She stood up, went to the kitchen and came out with a well-prepared dinner. Edyta was somebody who could smell good food from a distance. As Lucy opened the dish pot to dish out the food, the aroma drew him like a magnet toward the dining table. This made him salivate like a dog about to be served a meal by his owner. He came to the table, sat down without a word and started eating his dinner. Lucy was just watching him, and she knew right inside her that she loved this man and could do anything for him. Edyta finished his dinner, came to where Lucy was, held her hands and said, "What could I have done without you? Thank you so much for always being there for me, irrespective of all the odds."

He bent down, kissed her lips and said, "I don't know if it is the right time to say what I have been harbouring in my mind."

Lucy raised her head, looked him in the eyes and said, "Say it dearly; you know I do care for you."

Edyta kneeled and said, "It's a pity that I don't have an engagement ring with me right now, but I promise that once I go out, I will come back with it if you accept my proposal. Will you marry me?"

Lucy was amazed. She wanted to say yes, but instead, she started crying. Edyta reached inside his pocket, came out with a white handkerchief and wiped her tears.

"Will I accept your silence as yes, baby?" asked Edyta.

She said yes, and Edyta kissed her passionately. Lucy was breathing heavily. She had been dreaming of a day like this but did not know it would come so soon.

"I will be going out now to iron out things with Pete, and I promise you, once I come back, I will straighten things. We will plan how we will go on vacation; it's time to settle down and grow up like a man."

He kissed her again, collected his car key and left the room.

Trench was a bit hungry. He went to the kitchen, had a quick dinner, and came back to his duty post. As he was enjoying his dinner, he saw Edyta's gate open. He picked up his binoculars and saw the man on the steering wheel. He could not believe his eyes as he saw Edyta driving out of the bungalow. The drop of adrenaline entered his system as he could not hold his anger. His condition would not have been so bad if that animal had not disappeared with their money, the money the whole group fought so hard to get. He, once again, remembered how he had murdered Don in cold blood when he believed that he had a hand in the disappearance of the money. This was one moment in his life he hated to remember. All these were caused by this man he just saw driving out with one of the best cars in town. He told himself that sooner or later, he would make sure he paid for all the pain he had caused him. He dropped his binoculars, went to where Gudy was sleeping, woke him up and told him what he saw. Gudy jumped out of bed, looked at Trench and said, "Let's prepare and pay the bungalow a visit."

The two men hurriedly dressed up, carrying all they would need for the operation. Within a couple of minutes, they started walking along the street. At the back of Edyta's house was an under-construction building. Gudy discovered it a day before renting the apartment. Immediately after Edyta's house, there was a detour leading to the back of Edyta's house. They quickly crossed the road and located the bypass. They disappeared in the cover of darkness. The under-construction building had no gate but shared perimeter fencing with Edyta's property. To locate the property, Gudy produced torchlight from one of the bags he was carrying. He could see the open wall leading to the building. He went through the open wall with Trench following him. On reaching the back of the building, there lay the fence of Edyta's building. Gudy collected the gallon of raw acid he had bought from a motor battery dealer from Trench. He poured the whole of it on a small portion of the wall and waited. Neither of the two men talked to each other as they were just watching and waiting for the acid to affect the wall before they struck. When Gudy thought that the acid might have affected the wall, he produced a jack-knife from his bag and pressed his ear so hard to know if he could hear any sound or noise of people in Edyta's building. He could only hear a faint sound coming from either radio or television. He got satisfied and bent down to work. The effect of the acid had made the wall so weak. With the knife, he created a wide hole that could allow them to pass through to Edyta's compound. He entered first, and in front of him was a big rubber tank. He hid there, and Trench followed him. He gave Trench a sign to follow the other end of the building, carrying an automatic revolver Gudy gave him. With the gun in his hand, he grew in confidence, but Gudy had warned him not to shoot carelessly. He moved like a cat, and suddenly, they heard a door bang. Both of them stood still and flattened themselves on the wall. They waited for a moment. As no further sound was coming from the room, they became careful not to alert the gateman. At the other end of the building, the sound of the television was much louder in Gudy's ear. However, he ignored it and concentrated more on getting to the gateman. From where he was standing, he could see the gateman's house but no trace of the man. He paused for a while, looked at where Trench was coming from, and saw him hiding behind one orange tree on the far left side of the compound. He was closer to the gateman's house than Trench. He moved like a dangerous snake and found himself at the back of the building. He listened so carefully and heard a sound like someone was taking a bath. He moved closer to the entrance of the small house, and luckily, the door was ajar. He snicked in and went toward the sound of splashing water. There was no light in the room, and he did not bother to turn it on. He slowly went to the bathroom door; the door was closed.

The sound was much stronger now. He reached the handle of the door and opened it with no difficulty. Right in front of him was the gateman taking his bath. As Gudy entered the bathroom, the gateman noticed the presence of someone and shouted, "Lucy, is that you?"

There was no answer, and he reached for his towel, wiped his face, and turned on the light. Seeing a semi-automatic revolver pointing at him, he started shivering. He wanted to shout, but Gudy quickly went close, used the butt of the gun and hit him on the head. He went down without a sound. Gudy quickly undid the rope of the bathroom curtain and used it to tie up both his hands and legs, praying that his strike would not cause his death. Satisfied, he went outside and saw Trench by the door. Both entered the building. Trench followed him to where the gateman was lying down. He smiled and nodded to Gudy. They opened another door that led them to a small sitting room. It was not comfortable, but they managed it. Without wasting time, they offloaded all they came with. Gudy reached his front pocket, produced a cigarette packet, lit a cigarette from it, and threw the packet to Trench, who was already in dire need of a cigarette. He collected it and lit a cigarette from it.

Gudy said, "At least, so far so good. Let's wait for that animal to come back."

Both of them relaxed.

***

Cendy, lying in one of the unfurnished rooms in Edyta's house, had not tasted any food since she came into the room. She felt she was going to die, and the only person she was going to miss so much was her father. She was so much attached to her dad that her mother was always jealous of their closeness. Her mother once told her to get married and leave her husband for her. She knew that her father would not survive if he knew that she died in such a manner. And the irony of it was that none of her family members knew where she went to. She had to think of a way to escape from that place. Since she was brought into the room, she had not taken time to look around the room. All she had been doing was crying and wiping her tears. Her two hands were tied up, but not her legs. She stood up and walked close to the window. She saw a shadow that looked like that of a human being walk past; she looked closer and saw another image of a person coming through a wall with a gun in his hand. On seeing the gun, she left the window, went to the only plastic chair in the corner of the room and sat down. Had these two she saw come to rescue her? Indeed, she knew they were not her abductors. She wanted to shout, but she decided to keep quiet. She went to the door. It had no handle, but she believed that the door was locked. She saw another door at the left corner of the room, went there and saw that the door had a handle. She held the handle, and the door opened. The room was a bathroom with a shower and water closet. She looked around and discovered that the room had no window. She closed the door, came back to her cell, went to the door, and banged on it so hard.

Lucy jumped out from where she was watching television and came to the door. With a gun in her hand, she unlocked the door. She saw Cendy breathing heavily.

"What is eating you up, dear? Look, I'm in a good mood today, and I don't want you to spoil it for me. So you better behave yourself and don't touch that door again."

She closed the door, locked it, and went back to watch television. Cendy knew that she had a way of achieving her aim. She knew that those two men she saw had heard the sound. All she decided to do was to wait.

***

Pete was with his girlfriend when he received Edyta's phone call, and he discharged her with the promise that they would meet the next day. He drove to where Edyta was waiting for him. On getting there, he saw his boss in a joyful mood. He had been working for Edyta for many years, but he had never seen him in this kind of mood. He became so careful, knowing the kind of person he was. Seeing him coming, Edyta repositioned himself with a cup of Brandy in his hand and waved at him. Pete came to his table, greeted him, and sat down.

"Be happy with me, I just proposed to Lucy this evening, and she said yes. Ask the barman to give you whatever you would like to take. I'm just so happy."

Pete received the news with shock. Lucy was a very decent girl. What on earth had she seen in this crook? He was undoubtedly rich, but getting herself entangled with this man was something he could not comprehend. He congratulated his boss and wished him all the best. Edyta beckoned to the barman, "Take his order and bring one bottle for me. I'm just a happy man. My woman just said yes to my proposal."

The barman thanked him, left, and came back with Pete's order. Both men observed the table manners and were silent until they finished their meal. Their attention was drawn to a couple dancing to the melodious sound of music, 'Power of Love', by Celine Dion. Edyta sipped his drink, stood up and shook his waist to the rhythm of the music. Pete was looking at his boss like a total stranger. He knew Edyta as somebody who had never been in love. Edyta once told him that women are meant to serve men and that men are not meant to show affection to women because he believed that once you are rich, they will be attracted to you, like bees getting attracted to the nectar of the flower. He had to say something to commend his boss for the bold approach. He could not be sitting there without saying anything. Edyta would feel that he was not happy with him. He stood up and started dancing with Edyta. He embraced him and said, "Congratulations, boss. I'm so happy for you. All I'm asking is simple." Edyta's face brightened up, and he said, "Say it, and I will grant it at once. You don't know how happy I am today."

Pete came to him and whispered to his ears, "Sir, please, I will be happy if you consider me to be your best man."

Edyta stopped dancing, looked at Pete, sat down, picked up his cup of Brandy and said to Pete, "Do you know that it has never even occurred to me, but coming from you, I'm highly honoured. I will be going on a vacation with Lucy. Not only will you be my best man, but I will also be happy if you do the planning of my wedding."

Pete did not know that Edyta would agree to his request and was surprised that he had accepted him as his best man and his wedding planner. He had no choice but to accept it with happiness. He might benefit from it. Edyta finished his drink, lit his cigarette, and said, in a low tone, "My boy, I want to ask you one question, and I will appreciate receiving a candid answer from you. Darrel, my secretary, told me to my face that she overheard some people talking about me in Eddy's bar, that I'm into drugs and also a kidnapper. Apart from Lucy, you are the only person who knows me in and out of this city. I took you like a brother. Why have you betrayed me?"

Pete knew Edyta was up to something but did not know the direction he was coming from. He felt that all the talk of getting engaged to Lucy was just a decoy. He pretended he did not get him right, "Boss, to be Frank with you, I didn't understand what you meant when you said I betrayed you."

The joyful mood on Edyta's face had disappeared. Pete could see the real Edyta sitting right in front of him. What he had been sitting with before now was fake Edyta. Edyta wanted to raise his voice, but seeing a lot of people around, he controlled his anger and reduced his voice with a mean face that Pete scarcely believed was Edyta's, "What do you take me for, a fool? Who have you been talking to? Don't give me that innocent look. You know I'm a man you cannot toil with. I want the truth right now."

Pete cleared his throat and said, "Boss, you know me. I see you as my father, and you have been taking care of me since I met you. I have been highly benefited from you. I'm part and parcel of all your business. If I open my mouth so wide, I'm indirectly shooting myself in the foot."

He watched Edyta's reactions and knew that he was a little bit calm now. He continued, "This evening, I saw Randy in Eddy's bar. I bought him a drink, and he told me that a young chap was asking about you. He said the man was interested in knowing the kind of business you are doing, but he did not give him any useful answer. I thought he was only asking the question to be relevant. You know Randy; everybody sees him as notorious, and I did not take him seriously."

Edyta knew Pete was telling him the truth; besides, Pete had no reason whatsoever to lie to him because, just as he said, betraying him was indirectly shooting himself in the foot. Edyta did not trust anybody, and his previous plan was to use Pete and kill him, but proposing to Lucy changed the equation. He stood up, called the barman and paid for their drink.

"Can you follow me to my house? I promised Lucy that I would buy her a diamond ring when coming back, and as my best man, I want you to be a witness," said Edyta.

Pete had no other choice but to accord him respect and follow him. He left his car at the parking lot of the bar and entered Edyta's car. They drove to a jewellery shop in the city. He bought a costly diamond ring, went into a wine shop across the road, and picked a bottle of nice champagne for the celebration.

"Let's go and celebrate. I don't like keeping Lucy waiting."

They went to where they parked their car but did not notice one black Toyota Corolla parked not far from them. Tony had been following him from when he left his house to when he came to meet Pete. He had been on Edyta's trial. He saw the two men enter the jewellery shop and come out after a short while. He had already made up his mind that he was not going to let him out of his sight.

***

Kentus had not embarked on this type of mission before. He was only useful in providing security for his clients, mostly tourists who were new in town. He was so perfect in the job that he was even booked in advance. How they did that still baffled him until one day, he decided to ask one of his clients how he got his contact. The man simply said that he got it through his friend who had come to the city before. His friend highly recommended Kentus and talked well of him. Kentus could not hide his joy, and since that day, he believed in himself and increased his fees. He had been crushing on Sharon, but Sharon was a hard nut to crack. He knew he was embarking on this rescue mission to win Sharon's heart and also to improve his relationship with the police, which had gone bad. In the past, he had scuttled the police when he had an issue with one police undercover over his client. The problem lingered to such an extent that the chief of police had to step in and resolve the issue. But since then, his dealings with them had been like a cat and dog kind of relation. He knew that if he could get into the building, rescue Sharon's friend, and hand over Edyta and his gang to the police, they would have his confidence again and would not look into his affairs anymore. The previous day, he made arrangements for some bullets, which he already had. All he needed to do was to find a way to get access to Edyta's building and rescue the lady. He called Randy to ascertain if he had seen Edyta that evening, and Randy said yes. He told him that he was with Pete at that moment. So Edyta out of the way would make things so easy for him. On reaching Boulevard Street, he parked his car at the end of the road and with his gun under his jacket, he walked towards Boulevard Street.

Trench, finding it a little bit difficult to relax, went for his cigarette, picked one and lit it. His memory kept flashing back to how Don had begged him to spare his life, but he refused due to his suspicion that he connived with Edyta to divert their hard-earned money. He remembered it as if it was yesterday how he forced the barrel of his revolver into Don's mouth, squeezed the trigger and he died instantly. He promised himself that he would surely avenge the death of his friend, Don.

He went inside, came out with a bottle of Brandy, opened it, and took a mouthful of it. Gudy was watching him closely.

"Did you notice something when we were at the back of the house?" Judy asked.

Trench took his cigarette, looked at the burning end, dusted the ash, and said, "Yes, I guess someone is being kept captive there. But don't worry; sooner or later, we will figure out who the person is."

Gudy reached for the drink, took a mouthful, and closed his eyes.

***

Kentus, strolling towards Boulevard Street, looked at his wristwatch, and the time was 9.20 pm. He had never been to that street by that time; everywhere seemed so quiet, like a graveyard. He paused to make sure he was not being followed. On getting close to the building, he decided to hide in the well-maintained flower bed along the street to be double sure that nobody was following him. He was there thinking of what to do next when he saw the headlight of a car coming from the far end of the street towards his direction. He flattened himself on the flower bed. On getting close, he raised his head and saw two occupants in the car. He could not picture who, exactly, they were. He maintained his position, waited and watched the car. Getting to No. 7 Boulevard Street, the car stopped and blew the horn, but nothing happened. The driver blew the horn again; still, nothing happened. After the third blow of the horn, the gate was opened, the car disappeared into the compound, and the gate was closed gently.

***

Gudy glanced over his wristwatch and the time was 9:45 pm. He knew from the information he got about Edyta that he hardly stayed outside after 10 pm. He knew sooner or later that he would be coming home, and all the hell would let loose. He knew that getting the money from Edyta was not going to be easy. But no matter how difficult it was, he was not leaving his house without his money. His bank account was almost red, and he could not see himself going without the money. For him, it was a sin. He remembered all his promises to Darrel, and for him to fulfil all of them, he needed money. It was true he just met Darrel, but he had come to love her, and apart from that, age was no longer on his side. He had made up his mind to settle down once and for all. And all this required money. He took another gulp of the Brandy. With his gun in his left hand, he stood up and went where the gateman was and found out that he was shaking and trying to sit up. He brought out a sticky tape from his pocket, cut some length and used it to silence the gateman's mouth. He cut some again, tied his legs and hands, and was satisfied. He went back to where Trench was. As he was about to talk to Trench, he heard the horn of a car by the gate. Trench heard it, too, and stood up and they looked at each other. The horn blew again, and Gudy gave Trench a sign to go and open the gate. With his gun concealed at his back, he began to move towards the gate, and Gudy followed him.

Trench moved slowly towards the gate and saw through its pinhole that it was Edyta. He gave Gudy a sign. With Gudy's gun in his hand, he stepped backwards and hid inside the security room, leaving the door ajar.

Edyta was first to come down from the car with a bottle of champagne he was holding, followed by Pete. He was carried away by the event of the evening as he wanted to go inside to propose formally to Lucy. Because of this euphoria, he failed to notice that the person who opened his gate was not his gateman. It was Pete who saw it, but it was already too late. Trench, who locked the gate with a gun in his hand, was moving like a black mamba. Gudy, holding his automatic revolver, went straight to Edyta as Trench took care of Pete. He shot Pete in the head, and he died instantly.

"Remember what I told you back in the good old days: Wherever you go, remember the route that will lead you home. This is the end of the road for you," Gudy said in a very harsh tone.

As Edyta looked behind, he could not believe what he was seeing. The champagne in his hand slipped from his grip, smashed on the ground and blew like a bomb. The sound was so terrifying that even Lucy, who was in the kitchen cooking, heard the noise and ran out to see what was happening. Gudy smashed the butt of the revolver on his head, and he collapsed. Trench moved quickly with fantastic speed and used his gun to surround Lucy. Gudy pulled Edyta on his leg and dragged him inside the living room. Trench pushed Lucy inside the living room, too. With the sticky tape, they tied their legs and hands, and their mouth was not left behind.

"Where is the girl?" asked Trench.

He moved to Lucy, hit her across her eyes, and Lucy pointed at the door directly opposite Gudy. Gudy positioned his gun, moved to the door and opened it. Behold, Cendy was sleeping on the bed with tape wound around her legs. He woke her up.

Kentus, from his hiding place, heard the sound of something like gunfire followed by a sound like a bomb. He could not understand what was happening inside the building. He wanted to climb the mango tree to look into the compound. His nerves failed him. He went to his pocket and brought out a phone. He was about to dial his police friend's number when he saw another headlight coming in his direction. He paused, lying flat on his belly. The car stopped twenty feet from where he was hiding. He looked closely and recognized at once that it was Tony. He knew Tony very well, even though they were not too close. They had, a couple of times, drunk and smoked together. He stood up and moved towards the car. Tony had been following Edyta all day and had been driving at a safe distance so that Edyta would not know that he was being tracked. As Edyta drove across the lonely road with Pete in his car, he maintained his safe distance. On reaching another connecting road leading to Boulevard Street, he reduced the velocity of his car and put on his light indicator, heading towards his street. Tony still maintained his safe distance. At a range, Tony watched him stop at his gate, turned off the headlights of his car and waited.

Within a few minutes, the car disappeared into the compound. He considered two options: Either park his car on the adjacent street or drive to Edyta's gate. He chose the latter for easy escape. As he was still trying to negotiate a better place to park the car, through his inner mirror, he saw an image that looked like a human form growing out of the flower bed. He reached for his gun. As the image manifested from the well-trimmed flower bed, he observed the image further. Behold, he recognized, at once, the person. He returned his gun to where he usually hid it and waited for him to come.

***

Looking at Edyta lying on the bare floor, Gudy could not resist striking him again, but as he moved forward to hit him, Trench stopped him and said, “Boss, he won't need it now.” He left them and went to the kitchen. He came out of the kitchen with a cup of cold water and went closer to where Edyta was lying down. He poured all the cold water on his face, and he woke up at once.

Gudy looked around and saw one chair at the extreme corner of the room. He went there, drew the chair closer to where Edyta was sitting on the floor, and looked straight into his eyes, holding his gun casually.

“I will ask the question, and you will answer,” he said angrily.

He brought out his cigarette and lit it. There was a great silence in the room, except the only noise coming from an old clock hung on the wall. Edyta could not believe what was happening to him. He looked through his shoulder and saw Lucy sitting in the corner of the room, tied together with tape. Tears filled his eyes. He felt so sorry, for he knew that this was the end of the road for him and that their dream of becoming husband and wife would never come true. He knew that Gudy and Trench would never spare his life, so he made up his mind that no matter how hard they tortured him, he would never give them access to the money. He only had this thought in his mind, not knowing how prepared these two men sitting in his room were. If he knew, he would have thought of it twice. He wanted to cry but could not. As a thick ball of tears rolled down from his two eyes, he wiped it with his taped hand. As he wished and prayed for the inevitable conclusion, the ugly pain that normally tormented him any time in that situation came back again. It was like his heart was going to jump out of his mouth. He wanted to shout, but he could not. Lucy watched him closely from where she was sitting and wanted to stand up, but Trench timely reached where she was and slapped her across her eyes.

"Who asked you to stand up?" Trench asked her.

"He is going to die. Please, let me go and get his drug," she pleaded.

Gudy gave Trench a nod, thinking that what Lucy was saying might be true because, looking at Edyta, he knew something was not right with his health.

***

Kentus, on reaching Tony's car, opened the front car door and jumped inside, breathing heavily. He was sweating profusely, but the car air conditioner did the magic. Tony looked at him with keen interest and asked, "What are you doing here? I know you as a security guard, not a spy."

He explained to Tony how Sharon came to him as a friend to seek advice about her friend, who was kidnapped.

"I have been asking questions around, and all the indicators are pointing towards Edyta."

He went further to tell Tony that he was there last night on time to see Edyta drive in. He climbed one of the mango trees and overheard them talking about a lady and Sharon. So he came that evening to be double sure before alerting the police.

"But this evening, a lot has been happening in there. I heard a sound like a gunshot followed by another like a hand bomb. As I was about to call your boss, I saw a headlight coming. I think you need to call for backup at once."

Was he to believe the judgment of this man, or should he discard it and find a way to enter the building? A lot of thought was going on in Tony's mind. It's like a double-edged sword. If he went in there and made a mistake, his boss would never forgive him, but if he went in, subdued them, and got all of them arrested, he would become a hero.

"Are you sure of what you are saying?" he managed to say after a long pause while Kentus nodded. He went for his phone and dialled Tim's number.

***

Trench went where Lucy was and untied her. With the gun he was holding casually, he asked Lucy to get the drug. Lucy moved straight to Edyta's bed, opened the side bed closet, came out with a plastic container, opened it, picked two drugs and returned the vessel. Looking through her shoulder, she saw Trench watching every step of hers. He was lining on the door, admiring her. Because of the situation on the ground, taking her to bed was not a bad idea. He had not been with a woman for a very long time. His girlfriend had been turning him down because of what he did to her. He loved Kim very much, but the only problem with Kim was that he needed someone who could give him all the attention, which Trench did not. He got himself back and gave Lucy a sign with his gun to leave the room. Stepping out of the door, Lucy walked past him, moved to the kitchen, found a glass cup, went to the water dispenser, and fetched water there. She stepped out of the kitchen and went back to the living room. Gudy collected the water and drug from her. Trench guided her back to her position and tied her. Gudy forced the medicine and water inside Edyta's mouth, and he swallowed it. Trench produced a cigarette packet from his pocket, picked one cigarette from it and started smoking. Gudy gave him a sign to give him, and he threw the packet and the lighter to him. Both men were enjoying their cigarettes and waiting for Edyta to normalize. After a short while, the effect of the drug calmed his heart down. Gudy noticed it at once and poured the remaining water into the glass cup on his head and said, "You punk, I don't know the game you want to play here, but I assure you any kind of game you want to play, we are equal to the task. As I said earlier, all I want from you is simple answers. Let's get the ball rolling because we don't have that much time. Tell me honestly why you betrayed the group."

Edyta looked at Gudy's eye. What he saw gave him a shiver along his spine, but he had made up his mind not to play ball with these two. All he needed to do was to build his gut, resist all the punishment Gudy would give him, and wait for the worst. As for Gudy, a lot of things were going through his mind. Should he allow Trench to scuttle him a little, or should he gently follow this fool? He left them and went to the kitchen to find what he was looking for. After coming back, he looked for a socket, and when he found one near the television stand, he plugged the water-boiling rig into it and waited.

***

Tim was preparing to go to bed as he needed to be in the office much earlier the next morning. There was a case he was pursuing, which required his attention. He had been so busy in the office with a case that he did not even remember to check on Tony. But he knew that all was well with him, and if not, Tony, he knew, would have called him. He decided to call him before going to bed. He went to his bathroom, turned on the light, and had a quick shave. After that, he took his bath. When he was wiping his body with a towel, his phone rang. He had one old clock hung on the wall of his bedroom. He looked at it, and the time was 11.34 pm. Who might be calling him by that time? He tied the towel around his waist and went into his bedroom. He picked up his phone and saw that it was Tony calling. Tony was talking so fast on the phone.

"Sir, I'm at Edyta's gate at the moment, and I need backup. A lot is going on there," he hung up.

Tim, with his police knowledge, knew exactly what Tony meant, so he hurriedly went to his wardrobe, changed into something casual, and dialled a number. On the other hand, someone picked up at once.

"Arrange the boys pronto; I'm on my way. We are going for a ride."

"Yes, sir."

He locked his door, went to his garage, and drove as fast as he could toward the police station.

***

The boiling rig was hot red when Gudy unplugged it and came to where Edyta was. He gave Trench a sign to come and handed over the sticky tape to him. Trench collected it from him and used all of it to close Edyta's mouth. Satisfied! Gudy pressed the hot red boiling rig on Edyta's back, and it made a round mark. The pain was too much for him to bear. He wanted to scream, but no sound could escape the sticky tape. The smell of burnt skin was everywhere in the room. Lucy could not see the torture. All she could do was close her eyes and cry. Gudy went again with the rig. This time, the pain was just too much for him. He had uneasy feelings, and his strength was failing him. Edyta closed his eyes to see if he could control himself, but he could not because as he was closing his eyes, Gudy smashed his head with the boiling rig, and he fainted. Trench went into the kitchen, came back with a cup of cold water, poured the whole of it on Edyta's body, and he woke up at once.

"Listen very carefully; I hate to repeat myself. I will ask you the question once again, and I need the answer," said Gudy.

He bent down to remove the sticky tape on Edyta's mouth and gave Trench a sign to turn on the television, which he quickly did. He raised the volume to such an extent that it became difficult to hear Edyta's voice if he chose to scream.

"Why did you betray the group? I need the answer now."

Edyta could only see the movement of Gudy's lips, but he could not hear what he was saying as the pain in his back was too much for him. Trench came forward and kicked him severally on his ribs. He pulled him up and smashed the butt of his gun across his face. It gave him a nasty mark on his forehead, and blood was coming out of the cut. He pushed him down, and with a vicious rig, he went down, crashing his head on the hard marble floor tiles.

***

Tim was someone who hated to breach protocol. He was a diligent police officer who carried on his police job professionally, unlike other police officers who break the law every now and then. As Tim reached the police station, he parked his car at the car parking lot, and with a half-walk-half-run, he moved towards the office building. He met Jones at the entrance lobby.

"Where are the rest of the boys?" he queried.

"They are already waiting for you, sir," Jones replied.

"Good!"

He moved forward and quickly entered a room like a mini hall. All the boys were there, action-ready, and waiting for him. He quickly addressed them, and off they went to Boulevard Street. Then, he called Tony, and they talked for a few minutes. Tony looked at Kentus and said, "I told you that they would soon be here."

***

Trench came to Gudy, whispered to him, and Gudy gave him his approval. He moved slowly towards the kitchen. Within a couple of seconds, he came out with a kitchen knife and walked towards Lucy. Both Lucy and Edyta were watching him, knowing the type of person Trench was. Uneasy feelings enveloped Edyta. He knew that Lucy was vulnerable, and he equally knew that she could not bear the pain. He could not withstand seeing Lucy suffering at the hands of Trench. He knew that Trench was a beast which enjoyed torturing people. The ugly memories of what happened in the Contuoo region flashed back to him. He would not allow such treatment to befall Lucy. He had to do something to prevent Trench from inflicting body damage on her. Right inside him, the love he had for her had grown beyond his imagination.

Even though he knew that there was no way he was coming out alive from that mess, he had to come up with a convincing story that would make these two men shift their attention from Lucy. He gave a sign to Gudy to remove the sticky tape around his mouth. Gudy called the attention of Trench who was already holding Lucy's hand. Gudy retreated his step backwards and came to where Trench was. Trench told him to remove the sticky tape from Edyta's mouth. He moved close to Edyta with his gun in his hand and said, "You punk, if you play any games with me, trust me, I will eat your babe raw. So don't be stupid."

Holding his gun in his right hand, he used his left hand to remove the sticky tape.

Edyta looked straight into Gudy's eyes and said, "I'm ready to play ball, but I would like to drink water."

Trench raised his hand to hit him, but Gudy held his hand and asked him to go to the water dispenser, which was just around the corner of the living room. He quickly went to the water dispenser and opened the part that housed the disposable cups. He picked one up, fetched the water from the dispenser, came back, and handed the cup over to Edyta. Edyta drank the water slowly, buying time with it as his heart beat uncontrollably. He had been searching for the right words and stories to tell these two men, but his head was empty. After he finished drinking the water, he looked at Gudy and said, "All your money is intact. By tomorrow, we will go to the bank together, and I will transfer all the money to your account. All I want from you is to give me assurance that nothing will happen to my girl and me."

Trench went forward and struck him in such a manner that even Gudy did not see it coming.

"Look at me," Trench said, holding the collar of his cloth, "You have no right to give us condition. The moment you double-crossed the organization, you already sold your right."

Gudy pulled Trench away from Edyta, and both men stepped aside at the corner of the room and talked in a low tone. Gudy told Trench to calm down and allow him to handle the situation. He knew who Edyta was, and if they did not handle the situation well, they might end up having nothing. Trench nodded in approval, and the two men went back. Gudy searched into his pocket, produced a packet of cigarettes, picked one from it and lit it. He threw the packet to Trench, who was already badly in need of one, to calm his nerves. Both men smoked their cigarettes as if their life depended on it. All Edyta could do was to watch them and hope for the best.

***

Kentus was sweating heavily inside Tony's car. He brought out his half-soaked face towel and wiped his face.

"What is holding them? The station from here is not too far."

"Relax, my friend, very soon, they will be here."

As Tony was still talking, he saw, at the extreme far end of the street, the headlight of a car racing towards them.

"I told you they would soon be here."

Kentus heaved a sigh of relief, and both men came out of the car. Tim parked their car far away from where Tony's was. Tim came out with his special police automatic revolver, and the other boys, who were five in number, came out with their fully loaded AK-47 rifles. Without making a sound, they walked towards Tony.

As they reached where Tony and Kentus were, Tony briefed Tim on everything. Tim looked around and saw the mango tree close to the fence. He quickly climbed on top of it, and looking around the compound, he could only see what looked like a human shape lying on the ground. He could not see it clearly because there was no light. He contemplated using his torchlight, but on second thought, he decided not to use it. He kept on watching, but nothing more interested him. There were rays of light coming out of the window. He pressed his ear hard to know if he could hear any sound, but all he could hear was the sound which seemed to be coming from the television. He climbed down, took Tony with him, and asked others to hide under the flower bed. With his gun and a torchlight, he located the bypass adjacent to Edyta's fence. Both men walked silently into the darkness. As they walked within some metres, there was a detour leading to one uncompleted building. They quickly entered the building and traced their steps to the back of the building to locate Edyta's fence. With his torchlight, Tim could see a big hole made in Edyta's wall.

Tony could not believe what he saw. He said in a low tone, "May I go in, boss?"

Tim gave him a sign to wait and think of what to do.

"Go quickly and alert the boys to be vigilant and pick two boys there," said Tim.

Tony moved as directed by his boss and came back with two boys within a couple of minutes.

"Let's go in and pay them a surprise visit," directed Tim.

All four men, with their police automatic revolver rifles and the AK-47, entered the hole. First, Tim went into the compound. As he could see the water tank in front of him, he quickly took cover beside it and allowed others to come in. He gave Tony and Jones a sign to go through the right wing of the building as he and Duke followed the left side.

Silently, both men moved toward the front of the building. Tim and his men were the first to reach the front. There was a car parked on the far side of the entrance to the building. Tim tiptoed towards the car, and after getting to the car, he raised his head and saw Tony hiding beside a tree. Tim looked around, and close to him lay the lifeless body of Pete, covered with blood. Tim touched his neck and found it too cold and soon realized that he must have died over two hours ago. Tim moved like a black mamba towards the entrance of the building. On getting to the window, he pressed his head hard on the wall, and all he could hear was noise coming from the television. He raised his head, and looking through the window blind, he found a small opening that the window blind could not cover very well. With his Eagle eyes, he could see both Gudy and Trench holding guns in their hands and cigarettes in their mouth. He quickly moved out from there and came to where his men were. He gave Tony a sign to come. Tony and Jones crawled to where Tim was positioned. In a low tone, he told them what he saw.

***

With the cigarette in his mouth, Trench stood up, pacing up and down, as he could not understand why Gudy was treating Edyta with kid gloves. He had to devise a way to convince Gudy to let him rough-handle Edyta a little. Looking at Edyta, he could not resist pulling his trigger, but doing that would jeopardize all they came for. He had to find a way to control his emotions. He went to Gudy and said, "I think I need a drink. I have to go and get it."

Gudy wanted to stop him, but before he could do that, he had opened the front door. He stepped out and moved quickly towards the gateman's house. While walking past the parked car, he heard a sign from someone. He looked back and saw an automatic rifle pointed at his head. Tim gave him a sign not to shout. Tony dipped his hand inside his pocket, brought out a handcuff and handcuffed him at once. With alarming speed, Tim and the other two men rushed inside the building, surrounded Gudy at once and collected his gun without delay. Covering them all with their weapons, Tim asked Jones to ransack the entire building, which he quickly did. All of them were handcuffed, including Cendy.

Tim certified that there was no one in the building and instructed one of the boys to go in and check the gateman's house. He came to where Edyta was lying down with his handcuff, looked at his eyes and said, "This is the end of the road for you, my friend. You can run, but you can't hide forever. The arm of the law has caught up with you. Take him away."

He brought out his phone and called the paramedics to come with an ambulance. They took all the men and the ladies through the dark of the night to the Hilux truck parked at the end of the street.

9 788119 524600

Printed at Repro India Ltd.